Why are you asking me?

Let me think about it...

I DON'T RMEMBER EXACTLY!

Is there a reason you are asking?

I'M CURIOUS WHY YOU WANT TO KNOW.

IF YOU MUST KNOW....

Are you just trying to pick a fight?

Maybe I was
just shopping
for you!

I'm flabbergasted you need to know this right now...

You know i work too, right?

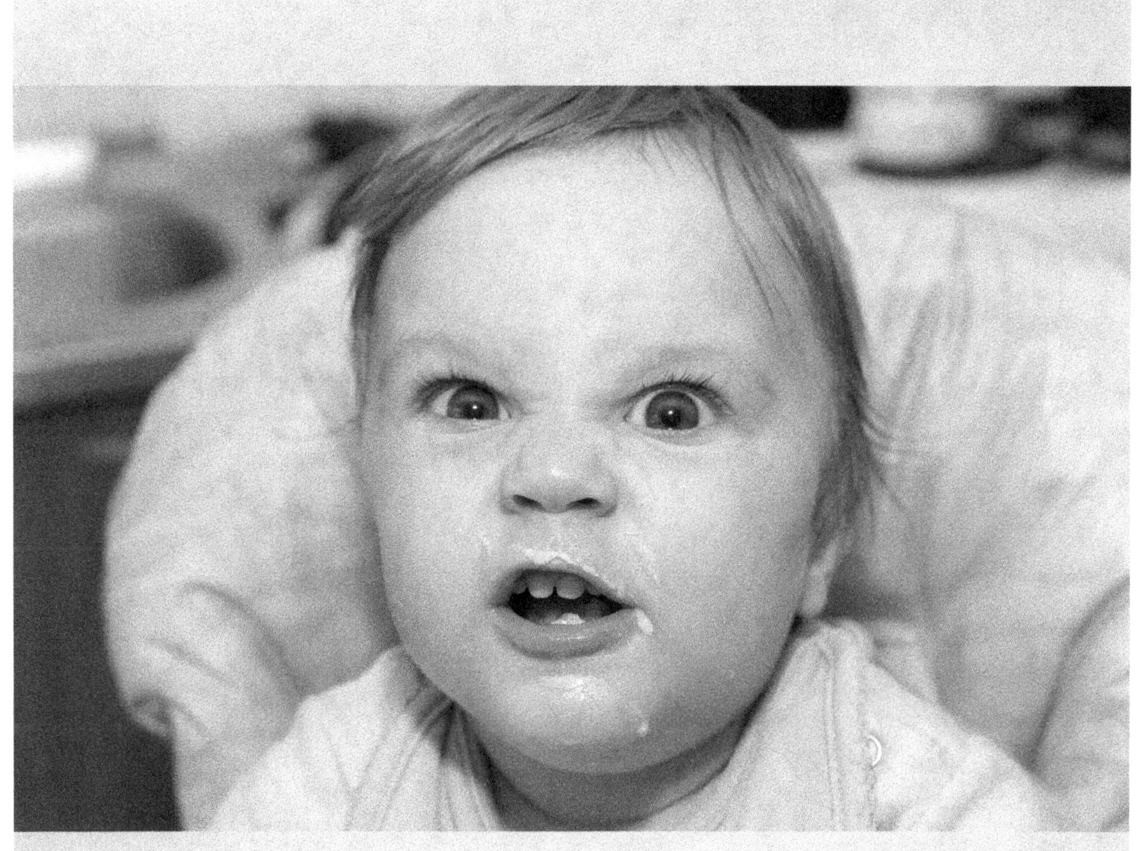

Did I ask how much you spend?

HUNTING SUPPLIES, FISHING, ALL YOUR HOBBIES?

Is this supposed to make me feel bad?

You seen how many boxes this month?

You really going
to ask me this?

Can I please enjoy my dinner?

NOW IS NOT THE TIME
TO DISCUSS THIS.

Would you believe I got some amazing deals?

Do you want me to return everything?

I feel like this is
an interrogation!

Are you mad?

Want me to start tracking what you spend?

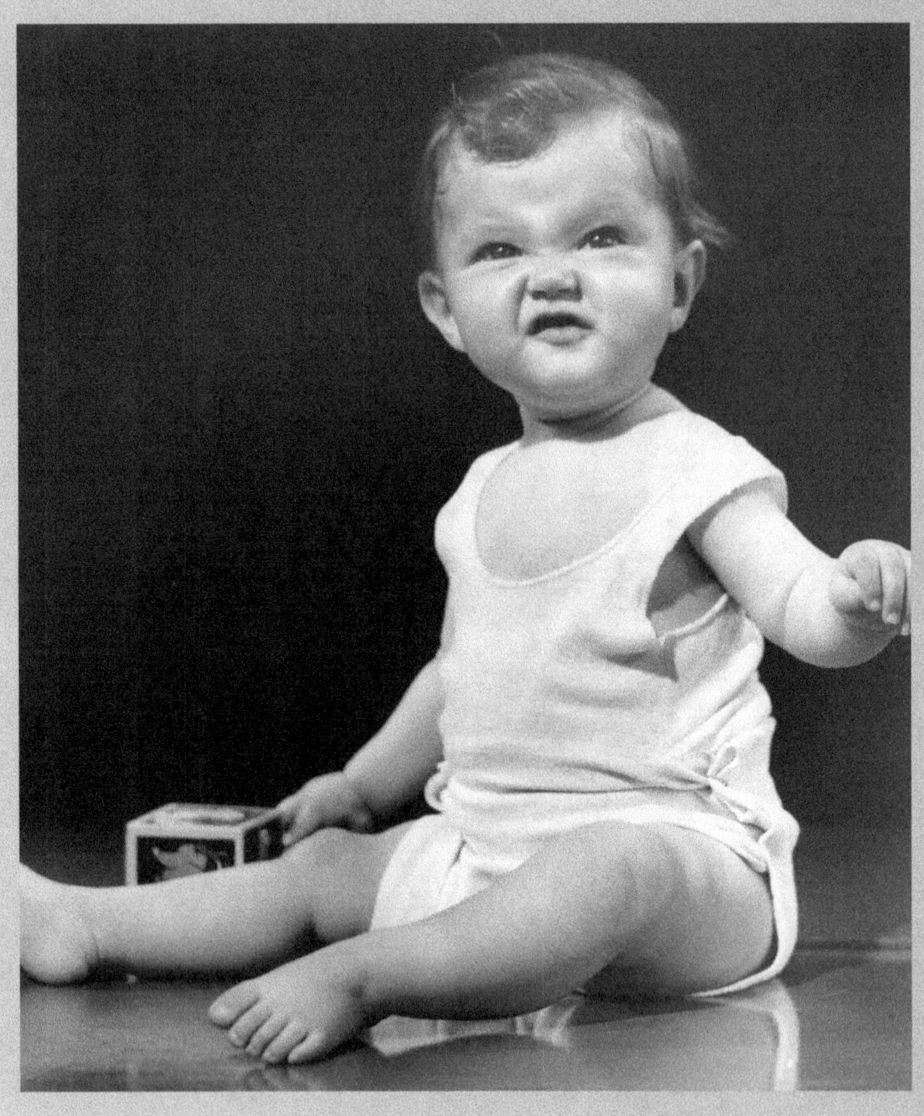

I really think this is irrelevant!

What new glasses and hat? I've had these!

That much?

I AM AS SHOCKED AS YOU ARE!

Our statement said what???

I don't know what you want me to say?

I was shopping
for the holidays!

Thank you!

WE HOPE YOU ENJOYED THIS GIRLFRIEND'S GUIDE. THERE WILL BE MANY MORE TO COME WITH SEVERAL TOPICS TO HELP A SISTER OUT. THANK YOU FOR SUPPORTING SMALL BUSINESSES!

www.ingramcontent.com/pod-product-compliance
Lightning Source LLC
LaVergne TN
LVHW080057170826
845677LV00024B/1781

* 9 7 9 8 3 5 5 3 3 7 3 9 1 *